Pete and Penny's
PIZZA PUZZLES

Case of the Secret Sauce

by Aaron Rosenberg
illustrated by David Harrington

PSS!
PRICE STERN SLOAN
An Imprint of Penguin Group (USA) Inc.

For Adara and Arthur, my own Penny and Pete.
I love you even more than pizza—AR

To my wonderful daughter, Emma—DH

PRICE STERN SLOAN
Published by the Penguin Group
Penguin Group (USA) Inc., 375 Hudson Street, New York, New York 10014, USA
Penguin Group (Canada), 90 Eglinton Avenue East, Suite 700,
Toronto, Ontario M4P 2Y3, Canada
(a division of Pearson Penguin Canada Inc.)
Penguin Books Ltd., 80 Strand, London WC2R oRL, England
Penguin Group Ireland, 25 St. Stephen's Green, Dublin 2, Ireland
(a division of Penguin Books Ltd.)
Penguin Group (Australia), 250 Camberwell Road, Camberwell,
Victoria 3124, Australia
(a division of Pearson Australia Group Pty. Ltd.)
Penguin Books India Pvt. Ltd., 11 Community Centre,
Panchsheel Park, New Delhi—110 017, India
Penguin Group (NZ), 67 Apollo Drive, Rosedale, North Shore 0632, New Zealand
(a division of Pearson New Zealand Ltd.)
Penguin Books (South Africa) (Pty.) Ltd., 24 Sturdee Avenue,
Rosebank, Johannesburg 2196, South Africa

Penguin Books Ltd., Registered Offices:
80 Strand, London WC2R oRL, England

ISBN 978-0-8431-9928-4   10 9 8 7 6 5 4 3 2 1

Chapter One

"One piping hot pepperoni pizza coming right up!" Mr. Pizzarelli called upstairs to his kids.

Penny hurried down. "Pizza for lunch again? Isn't there anything else?" she asked. She was only teasing. Penny loved pizza! After all, her family owned Pizzarelli's Pizza Parlor.

"Pizza time!" Pete shouted. He ran past Penny. She sighed. *Do little brothers have to get excited about everything?* she thought. *At least he can't be nine forever!*

Their dad laughed as they followed him through the kitchen and into the restaurant.

"Don't we get a puzzle with our pizza?" Pete asked. He loved pizza, but he loved puzzles just as much. Maybe more!

Mrs. Pizzarelli shook her head. She was tall and blond. Penny, who was eleven, looked like her. Pete was short and dark-haired like their father. "Pete, you sure take after your great-great-grandpapa. Papa Pietro loved his puzzles!"

"He used to leave clues and puzzles all over town for his family. Right, Dad?" said Pete.

Penny nodded. She loved to hear stories about her great-great-grandfather, Pietro Pizzarelli. He built the pizza parlor. And he was one of the first to live here in Redville. He even helped build the town.

"That's right," their dad replied. "Pizza and puzzles definitely run in the Pizzarelli family!" Mr. Pizzarelli often surprised Pete and Penny with puzzles of his own. Now he set a pizza slice in front of each of them. "Enjoy!" Then he went to wait on some customers.

"Pepperoni! My favorite!" said Penny. She reached for her slice, but Pete stopped her.

"Look!" he said, pointing at the pizza.

"What?" Then Penny saw it. "Hey!" The pepperoni formed lines across her slice.

"Dad must have done that on purpose," Pete said. He laughed. "Mine is like that, too! Let's puzzle it out!"

"Well, it looks like a picture," Penny said after a minute. "Like connect the dots. But I can't tell what it's supposed to be." Pete could tell Penny was getting frustrated. *She always wants things to make sense right away*, he thought. "Let's just eat," Penny said, picking up her slice.

"Wait!" Pete begged. "Let's try putting the slices together first."

"Okay, okay." Penny set her slice back down. Then she slid it over so the two slices were side by side. "That's it! All the pepperoni line up!"

"It *is* a connect the dots!" Pete said. Pete and Penny placed breadsticks on top of the pepperoni. Then they both stared at the image.

Connect the pepperoni without drawing diagonal lines.

(Answer, page 62.)

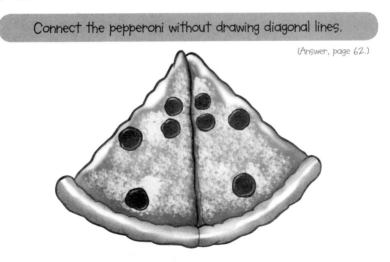

"What could the two rectangles be?" asked Penny. She turned the slices to look at the rectangles from a different angle.

"It looks like a suitcase," Pete said. "The smaller rectangle could be the handle!"

Just then their dad came back over. "Ah, you solved today's pizza puzzle!" he said.

"It's a suitcase!" Penny and Pete both said at once. They grinned when their dad nodded.

"But what does it mean?" Penny asked.

Their mother came out of the kitchen. "It means that your dad and I are going on a trip. We're going to Italy for the First Annual Pizza-Makers' Convention."

"Italy?" Penny asked. "Hooray for summer vacation!"

"Sorry, kids. Not this time," their dad said. "Who would watch the shop for us?"

"Yes, and who would take care of all our best customers?" added their mom.

Pete and Penny were disappointed they weren't going to Italy with their parents. But Penny had a question. "Does this mean you'll tell us how to make the secret sauce?"

"No, not yet," their dad said. "Not until you're older. You know that."

"That sauce recipe is very important," their mother added. "After all—"

"I know, I know," Penny interrupted. "Papa Pietro brought it over from Italy when he built the pizza shop. He taught the recipe to his oldest son, who taught it to his oldest son. Each one took over the restaurant. And then Grandpa taught it to Dad."

"That's right," Dad agreed. "And I promise I'll teach it to you and Pete when you're old enough to carry the secret."

"Hmph." Penny folded her arms across her chest.

"But if you don't tell us the recipe, how can we make our pizzas the right way?" asked Pete.

Their dad smiled. "Don't worry, I thought of that. I've written down the recipe for the grown-up who will be watching over you—and the shop."

Pete frowned. "Who's that?"

"Well," his mom answered, "since we can't take you to Italy—someone special has come here from Italy instead!" She pointed. Pete and Penny turned around. There was a short, round man standing by the door. He had shiny, black hair and a mustache with a warm smile.

"Hello, bambinos!" he shouted. *Bambinos* is Italian for *children*. Pete and Penny were off their stools in an instant.

"Uncle Gio!" They rushed over to hug him. Their Uncle Gio was one of their favorite

relatives. They didn't get to see him very often, though.

"You're going to run the shop with us?" Penny asked.

Uncle Gio smiled at her. "Yes! I'm staying with you while your parents are away."

Pete and Penny looked at each other. Uncle Gio was staying with them? They always had fun with him. This was going to be great!

Chapter Two

After the family finished lunch, Pete and Penny's parents headed out the door.

"Have fun!" Uncle Gio said. "Don't worry about us! Everything will be fine here!"

"Bye!" Mom called. "I love you! Be good!"

"Take care, kids!" Dad added. "We'll see you in a week!"

They had already hugged and kissed Pete and Penny several times. They kept coming back for one more good-bye.

"Go, or you will miss your plane!" Uncle Gio shouted to Mr. and Mrs. Pizzarelli. They nodded and got into their car. They waved as they drove away.

"There!" Uncle Gio said. "Now we get to work, eh?"

Pete nodded. Penny turned over the CLOSED sign and locked the door. "We have two hours before anyone shows up for dinner," Pete told Uncle Gio. "Dad closes the shop between lunch and dinner. That way we can get everything ready. Besides, there wouldn't be many customers during those hours, anyway."

"That's how it was when I last visited here, too," Uncle Gio remembered. He looked around the room. "This place even looks the same as it did back then."

Penny looked around the restaurant, too. She loved the way it looked with the old, wooden booths, bright walls, and checkered tablecloths. It was warm and comfortable. It was home. She didn't mind helping. She was happy that pizza was a part of their lives!

The pizza parlor was a lot of work, though. It was a favorite in Redville. Many townspeople ate lunch or dinner at Pizzarelli's. Some ate both!

Penny collected the plates and glasses left over from lunch while Pete tossed napkins, straws, and pizza crusts into the trash. Next he swept the floors and wiped down the tables. Penny washed the dishes. Uncle Gio was looking around the kitchen. He wanted to be sure he knew where everything was before he got started.

"Bambinos!" Uncle Gio called out. "Where are the pizza trays?"

"On the shelf above the oven," Penny said. That was where the circular metal trays were kept. That way her parents could easily reach them when they needed to make another pizza.

"There's nothing up there," Uncle Gio replied. "Nothing but this!" He was holding a sheet of paper. It had drawings on it. Uncle Gio handed the paper to Pete.

Pete studied it. "Neat! It's a rebus!" Of course his dad wouldn't go without leaving a puzzle behind! "That's a puzzle made of pictograms—when you use pictures to form words."

(Answer, page 62.)

He pointed at the top row. "That part says *beneath*."

Uncle Gio tugged on his mustache. "It does?"

"Sure." Penny pointed. "*Bee. Knee.* And then *tooth* minus *two* leaves only *th. Beneath.* Get it?"

"You bambinos are so clever!" Uncle Gio laughed.

Pete and Penny looked at the other pictures. The next one was someone shouting. There was a letter *o* after it. "*Yell* and *o*," Penny said after a minute. "I think that's *yellow*. Right?"

Pete nodded. "Right. *Beneath yellow* . . ." He looked at the next picture. "And this one's easy. That's a baseball *pitcher!*"

"*Beneath yellow pitcher.*" Uncle Gio scratched his cheek. "Hmmm."

Pete and Penny smiled. An old, yellow water pitcher sat on top of the kitchen cupboard. Penny looked inside the cupboard. "Here they are!"

She pulled out the pizza trays. Uncle Gio walked to the stove. A pot sat bubbling there.

"Ah, smell that sauce! *Delizioso!*" Uncle Gio said as he sniffed the sauce. He had a big smile on his face. "That's the famous Pizzarelli sauce all right!"

"Dad gave you the recipe for the secret sauce. Right, Uncle Gio?" Penny asked.

He smiled and pulled an envelope from his pocket. "I have it right here."

Pete and Penny stared at the envelope. The secret recipe! Uncle Gio had it in his hand!

Just then someone knocked on the front door. "I'll get it," Uncle Gio said. He set the envelope down and went to the door.

Pete and Penny stared at the envelope. Penny whispered, "We should open it!"

"We can't," Pete told her. "Dad gave it to Uncle Gio for his eyes only. Remember?"

"He's going to tell us the recipe someday, anyway," Penny pointed out.

"When we're older," Pete reminded her.

"Well, I *am* older!" Penny reached for the envelope.

"No!" Pete grabbed it from her. "Dad trusts us! So does Uncle Gio!"

"Uncle Gio left the envelope here," Penny argued. She took it back from Pete. "That means he won't mind if we open it!"

"No, it means he trusts us to leave it alone!" Pete said. He snatched the envelope.

"Give that back!" Penny said.

They both tugged on it at once. The envelope flew out of their hands. It sailed up, up, up. Then Pete and Penny watched as it fell right into the bubbling pot on the stove!

Chapter Three

Plop!

"Oh no!" Pete and Penny both peered into the pot on the stove. They could just make out one corner of the envelope. They watched it sink down into the very rich, very red, very hot sauce. It was gone.

"We have to fish it out!" Penny shouted. She grabbed a spoon and tried to get the envelope out of the pot.

"Aye, bambino, what are you doing?" Uncle Gio asked as he walked back into the kitchen with the mail. Penny set the spoon down quickly.

"Nothing," she answered. "I just wanted a little taste."

Uncle Gio glanced around. "Now where did I put that recipe for the secret sauce?"

Pete and Penny looked at each other. Then they gulped.

"It was an accident—," Pete started.

"It was my fault," Penny said. "I wanted to know the secret recipe. Pete tried to stop me. Then the envelope, well . . ."

Pete and Penny looked at the pot. Uncle Gio looked as well. "Aye, no!" He snatched the spoon and started stirring. "Now this whole pot of sauce is ruined!" After a second he lifted out the envelope. Pete and Penny watched as Uncle Gio peeled the soaked envelope apart. He laid the recipe on the counter. All three of them studied the paper. They could still read most of it.

But then they looked closer. "What's that?" Pete asked. He pointed to the last ingredient.

"It says one t-s-p," Penny answered. "That means *one teaspoon*. But I can't read the word that comes after that."

Uncle Gio gasped. He had realized something very important. "That's the secret ingredient!" He leaned against the counter. "Without that ingredient, I can't make more sauce. Without more sauce, I can't make more pizzas. Without more pizzas . . ."

"We're really sorry," Pete told him before he could say any more.

Penny nodded. She scuffed her sneaker on the floor. "I guess we'll have to call Mom and Dad. We'll just ask them to tell you the secret ingredient over the phone."

Uncle Gio shook his head. "They're on the plane already," he said. "And the convention is in an old monastery out in the country. There aren't any phones or computers. And cell phones don't work there, either."

"What about calling their hotel?" Pete asked.

"They're staying at the monastery," Uncle Gio answered. He sighed. "There is no way for us to get the secret recipe. And it's almost time for dinner." He tugged on his mustache. "Since this whole pot of sauce is ruined, we'll have to close the restaurant."

"What? No!" Pete held up his hands. "We have to stay open! Mom and Dad trusted us to keep the pizza shop going. We can't let them down now!"

"But how can we stay open?" Penny asked. "We don't have any pizza sauce!"

"Uncle Gio can make regular sauce," Pete told her.

"That's true," Uncle Gio agreed. "But I can't make the secret sauce."

Pete was thinking hard. "Maybe we can figure out the recipe on our own," he suggested. "Then Mom and Dad wouldn't even have to know what happened."

"And how will we do that, Mr. Smarty Pants?" his sister asked. Her hands were on her hips.

"Simple. We're only missing one ingredient, right? So we can try adding every ingredient in the kitchen, one at a time. Then we watch people's faces as they eat. If they love the pizza, then we'll know we got the secret recipe right."

Uncle Gio considered this. "It might work," he said. "I can change the last recipe ingredient each time."

"But people will be here for dinner soon," Penny reminded them.

Pete frowned. "We don't have time to experiment now. Uncle Gio, how fast can you whip up the regular pizza sauce?"

"In a jiffy!" Uncle Gio went to the spice cabinet. But he stopped when he looked inside.

"What kinds of names are these?" he demanded. "Last, usrag, peprep, cilrag, vleio loi, slabi? Is this a joke?"

"No, it's a puzzle—those are anagrams!" Penny told him. "Dad scrambled the letters of each word!"

"You're right," Pete said. "We should get a piece of paper to write down these wacky words. Then we can unscramble them."

Penny tore a piece of paper out of her notebook and handed it to Pete. He rewrote the letters as they were written on the jars. Then he drew lines below them so he could unscramble the words.

Pete climbed up on a stool and pulled down the container marked LAST. He started rearranging the letters on his piece of paper.

Unscramble the jars' labels.

(Answer, page 62.)

"This has to be salt." He opened the lid to look inside. "Yep!"

Pete and Penny got to work reading and decoding each label. Once they finished, Uncle Gio made the regular sauce.

He also made the dough and tossed it. Next he set it on the pizza trays. He added sauce and cheese. Then he waited to see which toppings customers wanted on their pizza slices. Pete and Penny took the orders.

The first customer was the town barber, Mr. Shears. He was even older than Uncle Gio!

"Ah, hello, Pete," Mr. Shears called out as Pete came over to take his order.

"Hi, Mr. Shears," Pete said, smiling. "What would you like tonight?"

"My usual," Mr. Shears replied. "Sausage, pepperoni, and black olives. So, Pete, there was this one time when I was a boy . . ."

"Sorry, Mr. Shears, can't chat now!" Pete said. He hurried back into the kitchen. He liked Mr. Shears, but the old man loved to talk. Pete avoided walking past his barbershop. Otherwise, he'd be stuck listening to his stories for hours!

"One sausage, pepperoni, and black olives," he called out. Uncle Gio nodded. He tossed the toppings onto the slice. Then he used one of the long-handled wooden platters to slide it into the oven.

Penny got the next customer.

"Hello, dear." It was Ms. Green. She owned Redville's grocery store, Vera's Veggies. "How are you today?"

"Fine, thanks," Penny answered. "What can I get for you? The usual?"

"Oh, yes, thanks." Ms. Green always had a slice with vegetables on it. "Are you eating enough veggies, Penny? They're super-delicious and nutritious!" Ms. Green thought Pete and Penny ate too much pizza and not enough vegetables.

"Yes. I'm eating my veggies, Ms. Green," replied Penny.

Several other locals turned up for dinner. So did a few people who were simply driving through town. That was no surprise. Pizzarelli's Pizza Parlor was one of the best restaurants in Redville!

The visitors seemed to enjoy their pizza. The local townspeople, however, were not quite so easy to please. They had eaten at Pizzarelli's often enough to know that this sauce just wasn't right.

"Something seems a bit different tonight," Mr. Shears said. "This pizza lacks its usual zest."

"It doesn't taste quite right," Ms. Green said. "I think the sauce tastes a bit funny."

Mrs. Crier was more direct. "That uncle of yours doesn't know what he's doing!" Mrs. Crier was the town gossip. She owned the Redville beauty salon, the Perfect Look. Her long nails and poufy, blond hair were always perfect. But Pete and Penny often thought her attitude needed some help!

"I know, I know," Uncle Gio said sadly when Pete told him what the customers were saying. "It's the sauce! Without our secret sauce, the pizza is just . . . plain. It's not special!"

"We really need to find that secret ingredient. And soon!" Penny said.

The three of them looked at one another. The hunt was on!

Chapter Four

The next morning at breakfast, Pete was still worried. "If we don't think of something soon, people will stop eating here. You heard what the customers said last night!"

"Maybe we should tell people what happened," Penny suggested. "The truth."

"What?" Pete almost fell off his stool. "Are you crazy?"

"No, listen." Penny set down her orange juice. "We should tell the regular customers we're testing sauces. They're our friends. And they all know what our secret sauce *should* taste like. So they can help by telling us if we're getting close!"

"That's true," Pete admitted. "And if they know what happened, they won't be mad that the pizza doesn't taste as good."

Penny nodded. "We could even make it into

an event," she suggested. "The Pizzarelli Pizza Puzzle! Anyone who participates will get free pizza."

Pete thought about it. Then he grinned. "We'd have a whole town of sauce tasters!"

"What's this?" Uncle Gio had gone out front to get the newspaper. "A town of tasters?"

They told him their idea.

"I like it, bambinos!" Uncle Gio gave them a warm smile.

After breakfast, Pete and Penny got to work. They drew flyers for the Pizzarelli Pizza Puzzle event. They made copies at the library. Then they called all their friends. The other kids loved the idea. They especially loved the part about free pizza! They each took a stack of flyers to put up around town.

The first lunch customer was Mr. Parcel. He was Redville's postman.

"Good day, young Pizzarellis!" Mr. Parcel said as he walked in the front door. "I brought your mail. I also brought my appetite—and a riddle!" Pete and Penny liked Mr. Parcel. He was always cheerful and friendly. And he almost always brought them a riddle to solve. Most of them had to do with the mail.

"Hi, Mr. Parcel," Penny replied. "Did you see our flyer?"

"I did." The postman sank into his usual booth. "And I'm happy to help."

Penny smiled. "Thanks! The pizza will be ready in a few minutes. Just tell us if the sauce tastes right."

"Of course!" Mr. Parcel slapped the tabletop. "Bring on the pizza!"

"But what's our riddle?" Pete asked. Penny might have forgotten about it, but he hadn't!

"Oh, yes," Mr. Parcel said. "What's black and white and red all over?"

"A newspaper, of course!" Pete quickly replied.

"Yeah, everyone knows that," Penny added.

"Not so fast," Mr. Parcel said. He smiled and proudly held up a piece of his own mail. "This envelope—after yesterday's lunch at Pizzarelli's!"

The kids laughed. The envelope was splattered with sauce.

Elliot and Rupert Jest showed up next. The brothers owned the town's toy store, Jest Joking. Pete knew they were grown-ups, but most of the time he thought they acted like big kids. They made everyone laugh.

"No more secret sauce? Oh no!" Elliot moaned. He threw himself down face-first on the table.

"There, there." Rupert patted his head. "We'll get through it somehow."

Pete and Penny looked at each other. Was Elliot really *that* upset?

"What will we do?" Elliot wailed. His head was still on the table.

"Well," Rupert said, scratching his chin, "I guess we'll just have to keep eating until the slice is right!"

Boing! Elliot bounced back up. He had a huge grin on his face. "Count me in!" he declared.

Pete and Penny laughed. Two more test subjects! The lunch rush was just beginning.

In the kitchen, Uncle Gio was working hard. He couldn't make one big vat of sauce like he normally would. Instead he had six saucepans on the stove.

"One sauce has white pepper in it," he told Pete and Penny as he pointed to a pan. "And that one has chili powder. That one there has lemon peel. One has sugar. I added ginger to one. Oh, and that one has orange juice!"

"Great!" Pete looked at the saucepans. "How do you remember which is which, though?"

"Heh!" Uncle Gio twirled his mustache. "You're not the only one who knows a thing or two, bambino! I made a secret code!" He pointed at the pans again. Each one had a piece of tape on its handle. There was a number written on each piece of tape.

"You used a code? Cool!" Pete studied the numbers.

Uncle Gio started singing something in Italian and went back to work. Pete and Penny looked at the numbers on the pans. Each number had to match an ingredient. But how?

"What ingredients did he say he used?" Penny asked as she took out her notebook.

"White pepper, chili powder, lemon peel, sugar, ginger, and orange juice," said Pete. Penny wrote all the words down in a list.

"And the numbers are nineteen, twelve, seven, three, fifteen, and twenty-three," Pete added. Penny wrote each number down on the same piece of paper.

Pete grinned. "I bet the numbers represent the first letter of each ingredient! That saucepan has a three on the handle. And *c* is the *third* letter in the alphabet, so that must be the chili powder!"

Penny laughed as she drew a line to connect chili powder to the number three. They solved the other saucepan mysteries. "We figured out the code!" she told Uncle Gio.

Connect each ingredient with the correct number on the list.

(Answer, page 62.)

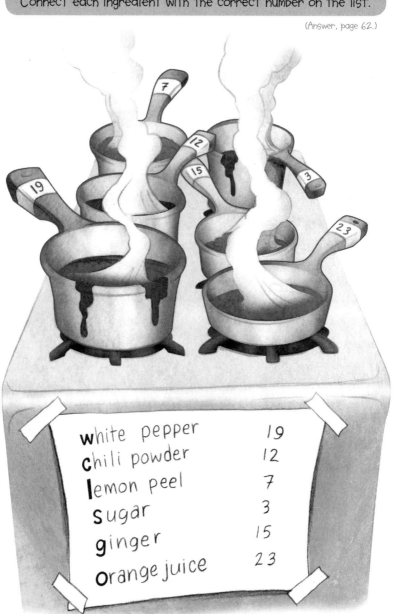

white pepper   19
chili powder   12
lemon peel   7
sugar   3
ginger   15
orange juice   23

"Good work!" said Uncle Gio. He placed the slices into the oven in numerical order. He didn't want to mix them up. "Papa Pietro would be proud!"

Pete and Penny beamed. They liked the idea that Papa Pietro would have admired their puzzle-solving skills.

Then Uncle Gio pointed to an old rolling pin sitting on the counter. "Did you know that was Papa Pietro's rolling pin? He made it himself!"

Pete and Penny stared at it. They had seen that rolling pin every day of their lives. But they never knew it had belonged to their great-great-grandfather!

"Wow," Pete whispered.

Uncle Gio slid several slices out of the oven. He put them onto serving trays. "Now it's time to puzzle out this secret recipe!"

"Absolutely!" The kids grabbed trays. Penny headed to the booths. Pete was right behind her.

The customers eagerly ate their slices. Pete and Penny waited to hear what they thought. The news wasn't good.

"*Aa-choo!*" Mr. Parcel sneezed. Then he sneezed again. "I don't think that's it! *Aa-choo!*" He had white pepper in his sauce.

"It's interesting," Elliot said. "But it's a little too sweet. And the cheese keeps sliding off." His sauce had orange juice in it.

"I like it," Rupert claimed, coughing. He reached for his water glass and took a big gulp. "Could I get some more water, please?" His face was turning red. Tears were streaming down his cheeks. Chili powder was in his sauce!

"I like sugar just fine," Mrs. Crier insisted, "but not on my pizza!" She made a face.

"It wasn't quite right," Mr. Shears agreed. His sauce had ginger in it.

"Mine was a bit tart," Ms. Green offered. She looked like she'd sucked on a lemon. In a way she had. Her slice had lemon peel in it!

"None of the sauces were right," Pete told Uncle Gio later. All the customers had left. And there were many unfinished slices in the trash.

"Don't worry, bambino," Uncle Gio said. He smiled and patted Pete on the back. "We'll figure it out. Why don't you help me roll out the dough for dinner?"

Pete cheered up. "Can I use Papa Pietro's rolling pin?"

"Absolutely!" Uncle Gio handed it to him.

Then he went to gather more ingredients.

Penny returned to the kitchen. She had been cleaning up. "What are you doing?" she asked her brother.

"I'm going to help roll out the dough," Pete said. "And Uncle Gio said I could use Papa Pietro's rolling pin!"

Penny pouted. "But I want to use that pin!"

"You can next time. I get to this time." Pete held the rolling pin to his chest.

His sister grabbed one end. "Just let me try it for a sec!"

"No!" Pete tugged on his end.

"Let go!"

"No, you let go!"

Then there was a loud *snap*.

Chapter Five

"Oh no!" Pete moaned. "Not again!"

Uncle Gio rushed into the kitchen. He stared at Pete and Penny. They stared at their hands. They each held one handle. The rest of the rolling pin lay on the floor between them. "What happened?" asked Uncle Gio.

"We broke it," Penny said sadly. "I'm sorry! It was my fault!"

"Again," Pete pointed out.

Uncle Gio was studying the rolling pin. He held out his hands. "Give me your pieces," he said gently. Pete and Penny gave him the handles. No one said a word.

"I don't think it's broken," Uncle Gio said after a minute.

"Really?" Pete asked. "But the handles came off!"

"I think they were meant to." Uncle Gio

showed him the rolling pin. Then he showed how one handle fit perfectly back into place. He even twisted the handle back off again. "It looks like it was made to come apart."

Penny gasped. "Can I see that?" she asked. "Please?"

Uncle Gio handed her the rolling pin.

Penny turned it. She looked into the hole where the other handle should go. Yes! She *had* seen something in there! "Look at this!" She stuck her fingers in carefully. Then she pulled out a rolled-up piece of paper!

"A hidden compartment?" Pete was amazed. "The rolling pin was built like a puzzle box! We must have tugged on it just right to open it!"

Penny grinned. For once her temper had led to something good!

The paper looked very old.

She carried it to the table and carefully unrolled it. Pete and Uncle Gio were right behind her.

"It's a maze!" Pete said. Penny rolled her eyes. She could see that it was a maze! But why had Papa Pietro put a maze inside his rolling pin?

"That's our pizzeria," Uncle Gio said. He pointed to a picture in the bottom corner. "What's this?"

"It looks like Pierpont Pond," Pete said. He pointed to another drawing. "And that's the old schoolhouse. And there's the cemetery."

"This one in the center must be the town square." Penny tapped the last drawing. "Papa Pietro must have wanted to lead us somewhere. Now we just have to solve the maze to figure out where. I'm guessing we should start from where *we* are—the pizza parlor!"

"Right!" Pete pulled a pencil from his pocket. "Let's puzzle it out!"

He started tracing a route from the pizza parlor. Penny and Uncle Gio made suggestions. This was tough. It was a good thing he was using a pencil! Finally Pete traced his way through the maze.

Solve the maze.

(Answer, page 62.)

40

"That's it! Now we know where to go!" he shouted.

"But what does it mean?" Uncle Gio asked.

"I don't know," Pete admitted. "Let's head over there to see what we can find!"

Uncle Gio nodded. "You bambinos go ahead and see where your puzzle leads," he told them. "In the meantime, I'll try out some more test sauces!"

Penny headed for the door. Pete carefully rolled the paper back up and slipped a rubber band around it. Then he hurried after her.

Chapter Six

Pete had to walk quickly to keep up with Penny's long legs.

They saw several townspeople as they walked to the town square. Each one said hi. Pete and Penny had always liked living in Redville. It was such a friendly town!

Pete especially loved it because it was such a quirky town. How many towns had a street that intersected itself? Pete and Penny had just turned left off of Main Street *onto* Main Street! Redville even had a street that changed its name every few blocks. And each name started with the next letter of the alphabet! Penny's favorite blocks were where Apple Street turned into Blueberry Street.

Visitors got confused all the time. But Pete and Penny had grown up here. They knew exactly where they were going. Besides, they knew

Redville was unique because Papa Pietro had helped design it. He had turned the whole city into one giant puzzle!

They soon reached Redville's Town Square. It was a big, open square with a one-way street on each side. A grassy park took up most of the square. A statue of Gregory Red, the town's first mayor, stood at the center.

"Now what?" Penny wondered. She and Pete looked around. Some of their friends were out playing. They waved to Pete and Penny. Pete and Penny waved back. But the two of them were too busy to play with their friends.

"Let's look at the drawing again," Pete suggested. He unrolled the paper. They both studied the tiny drawing of the town square. "Let's try looking over there first."

They headed across the square. A man was walking toward them. It was Captain Bell, the chief of police.

"Hello, Pete! Hello, Penny!" Captain Bell was a tall, stocky man with a wide face and short, black hair. He always had a big smile. "Out for a bit of fresh air?"

Pete glanced at Penny. She nodded. "We're actually looking for something." They showed Captain Bell the maze. "We don't know what we're looking for, though."

"Hm." Captain Bell rubbed his nose. "By the way, how's your Pizzarelli Pizza Puzzle event going? Mrs. Crier told me the test sauces weren't such a hit."

Pete wasn't surprised that he'd heard. Mrs. Crier was such a gossip!

"All right, thanks," Penny said. She looked down at the maze and tapped the piece of paper. "Do you happen to know what this is trying to show us?"

The police chief studied the paper. "Wow. This is old," he said after a minute. "Hmm. The drawing looks funny somehow."

Pete and Penny stared at the picture again. Then Penny gasped. "The statue! It's missing!"

Pete shook his head. He was amazed he hadn't noticed. It made sense, though. Papa Pietro had lived here long before that statue was built.

"So what *is* still here from back when Pietro was alive?" Pete asked.

"Just the park grounds," Captain Bell replied. "Oh, and the bricks at the center. They were part of the original town square."

They looked down. The ground around the statue was made of old brick. Then Pete remembered something. "These bricks have names on them, don't they?"

"That's right," Captain Bell said. "Each brick

has the name of one of the town's founders written on it."

Pete and Penny were already studying the bricks. They had both had the same idea. "I found it!" Penny shouted a few minutes later. She kneeled down to get a closer look. The brick's worn letters read PIZZARELLI.

"Great!" Pete dropped to his knees and felt along the brick. "This has to be what he meant for us to find!"

"Now what?" she asked.

"I don't know," Pete said. "Can we pull it up?"

"Don't even try," Captain Bell warned. "That brick has been there a long time!"

Pete tested the brick with his fingers. It wouldn't budge. "Moving it isn't the answer." He frowned. "But what is?"

Penny was already getting frustrated. "Maybe the answer's somewhere else," she said, looking around.

"No, this has to be it," Pete insisted. "Look harder!"

"Hello, Pizzarellis!" Mr. Shears had just stepped out of his barbershop. The shop was on one of the streets beside the town square. "What have you found there?"

"Hi, Mr. Shears," Pete answered. "It's just a brick with our family name on it."

Penny nudged her brother. "That's not *all* it is!" She pointed. "Look at these marks! They're under each letter of our last name!"

Pete leaned in for a closer look. "Those marks can't be there by accident," he said. "They look too neat. And there are more under some letters than others. It has to be a message!"

He searched his pockets and pulled out a pencil and his notebook. Then he counted the notches under each letter. He wrote those numbers down.

"Sixteen, twenty-two, nineteen, twelve, ten, twenty-one, four, nine, six, and fifteen," he read when he was done. "It has to be a numbered code. Each number must mean its own letter. But there are more notches under one *Z* than the other. How will we figure out which letter goes with the number one?"

Penny went back to examining the brick. As usual, she didn't care for her little brother's puzzling-out lectures. "You counted wrong," she told him. "There are twenty marks by the first *Z*. You said nineteen."

"Yes," he agreed. "But one mark is above the *Z*. The other marks are below it. So I didn't count that one." Then his eyes widened. "That's it! Papa Pietro marked that one on top to show us which letter to start with! *Z* must equal one! That means the other *letters* of 'Pizzarelli' don't really matter. We just use the Z=1 code breaker to decode the rest of the *numbers* in the message!"

Decode the message. (Use the secret code in the front of this book!)

(Answer, page 62.)

PIZZARELLI

Count the dots. Write the numbers on the lines above.

Using the secret code, write the letters on the lines above.

Penny was happy *she'd* found the answer—well, sort of. Pete quickly worked out the rest of the letters. He wrote down each one as he figured out the code. It was easy now that he knew Z=1! He showed Penny the answer when he'd finished.

"Our kitchen?" Penny read. "What does that mean?"

Pete grinned at her. "Don't you see? Pietro is saying that the next clue is hidden in his family's kitchen!"

Penny stared at Pete. "But he built the pizzeria. He lived above it, just like us. And we don't have a kitchen upstairs. We just use the restaurant's kitchen. Wouldn't that mean—"

"Exactly!" Pete climbed to his feet. "Come on! The secret, whatever it is, is in our kitchen!" He took off running. Penny raced after him.

Chapter Seven

"Is that you, bambinos?" Uncle Gio called as Pete and Penny returned to Pizzarelli's.

"Yes, it's us!" Pete called back. He and Penny hurried into the kitchen.

"How did it go?" Uncle Gio asked. He had pizza trays out. He was tossing pizza dough while he talked. "Did the maze lead to anything?"

"Another puzzle! And that led us back here," Penny replied. "Whatever Pietro wanted us to find is in this kitchen."

"How did it go with your test sauces?" Pete asked, changing the topic.

Uncle Gio shook his head. "None of them were right," he answered. "But I'll keep trying." He smiled. "So Papa Pietro hid something in this kitchen, eh?" Uncle Gio said, getting back to the puzzle.

"Check everywhere," Pete told them.

"Anything could be a clue."

He and his sister began searching all over the room while Uncle Gio went back to making pizzas. Pete was studying the cabinets and the countertops. Penny was looking at the furniture and the floor. Nothing looked like a clue. Then Penny noticed the painting hanging on the wall.

Penny gasped. "I think I found it!" She pointed to a portrait of Pietro Pizzarelli.

"What makes you think the clue leads to that?" Pete asked.

OUR KITCHEN

Penny pointed to a small plaque at the bottom of the frame. It read OUR KITCHEN. "That's what the brick said, too!" she explained. "It has to be our next clue!" She frowned. "He wanted us to see this. But it's just a painting. What can it mean?"

Pete wasn't listening to Penny. He was too busy staring at the portrait. "It is definitely the same kitchen," he said slowly. "But something is different." He pointed to the painting. "Look behind Papa Pietro." All three of them leaned in to look. Pietro Pizzarelli was in front of the pizza oven. And on top of the oven sat a glass jar.

"That's weird. Dad never lets us put anything right on top of the oven," Penny said.

"And Papa Pietro would know never to do that," Uncle Gio pointed out. "The oven is too hot. A glass jar would shatter!"

The three of them crowded closer to the painting. It was hard to see because the jar was so small. They could just make out the jar's label. But it didn't have words on it . . .

"It's another rebus!" Penny said.

"Can you two figure it out?" Uncle Gio asked.

(Answer, page 62.)

Pete squinted to look at the first pictogram. "That's a man mowing grass," he said. "So that could be *mow*. The next one is a drawing of a girl. And then there's an *S*." He scratched his head. "Mowgirls?"

Penny laughed. "No, silly! Who's ever heard of something called mowgirls?" Then her eyes got wide. "The pony book I'm reading right now is set in Scotland. And they keep calling the girl character a *lass* or *lassie*."

Pete grinned. "Good thinking, Penny! *Mow*, *lass*, plus the letter *S*. Of course! It's *molasses*!"

"Molasses! Wait a minute! That must be the secret ingredient!" Penny said. She was hopping up and down with excitement. "Papa Pietro was showing us how to make his secret sauce!"

"That makes sense," said Pete. "He knew our family's secret recipe could never be lost as long as the picture was still here! And there's no way a non-Pizzerellian could have puzzled this out!" He thought of something else. "Hey, there was a jar in the back of the cabinet—the name on the label started with *mo*. I bet that's the molasses."

"The answer's been right in front of us all along?!" cried Penny.

Uncle Gio had a huge smile on his face. "We will have Pizzarelli's secret sauce bubbling in no time!" he said excitedly as he went to the cabinet.

Soon it was dinnertime. Pete and Penny served up the first few slices using the new sauce.

"Now that's more like it!" Mrs. Crier said. She delicately wiped her mouth with a napkin.

"Perfect! You kids sure nailed it," Mr. Parcel happily agreed.

"Excellent slice," Mr. Shears said. He patted

his belly. "That reminds me of the time—"

"I don't think I've ever had a better slice of pizza," Elliot Jest claimed.

"Easy for you to say," Rupert complained. He glared at his brother.

"What's wrong?" Penny asked him.

"He stole my slice!" Rupert whined. He sounded just like a little kid!

"It's not my fault you don't eat fast enough," Elliot said. He laughed.

"Don't eat fast enough? I'll show you fast eating." Elliot was wearing a tie shaped like a fish. Rupert grabbed the end and started chewing on it.

"Let go!" Elliot shouted. But his brother kept on chewing.

Pete and Penny laughed. They were happy they had found the secret ingredient. Now everything at the shop would be okay. They looked around the crowded restaurant. The Pizzarelli Pizza Puzzle event had brought in lots of new customers. But with all the drama, Pete and Penny wondered if their parents would regret having left them in charge . . .

Chapter Eight

A few days later, a woman stopped by for lunch. She said she was new in town, and introduced herself as Ms. Scoop.

"I heard about what happened," she said after eating a slice with black olives. "Mrs. Crier said you lost your family's secret recipe!"

Penny sighed. *Mrs. Crier really is a horrible gossip!* she thought.

"That's true," Penny admitted. "But then we found it again."

"You had to search for clues, though, right?" Ms. Scoop asked. "I hear you found one on a brick in the town square."

"We did," Pete agreed. He had wandered over to the booth. "Our great-great-grandfather left clues so that our family's secret sauce ingredient would never be lost."

"I'd love to hear all about it!" Ms. Scoop said.

She leaned forward eagerly.

Pete and Penny took turns telling her what had happened. They told her about dropping the envelope into the sauce. They talked about trying different ingredients the next day. Then they talked about the rolling pin. They explained how Penny had found the maze. They told Ms. Scoop how they had wound up at the town square. And about the code on the brick. They even told her about the final clue being in their very own kitchen. The only detail they left out was noticing the jar in the painting and decoding the secret ingredient. That would stay a Pizzarelli family secret!

"That's a great story. And this pizza sure *is* scrumptious," Ms. Scoop said when they had finished. "I'd love to write an article about it. Would that be okay with you?"

Pete and Penny were shocked. They turned to Uncle Gio. Ms. Scoop explained that she was a new reporter for the *Redville Gazette*. Uncle Gio nodded.

"No one else will be able to figure out our secret recipe from what you said to Ms. Scoop," he told Pete and Penny. "And you deserve some credit for being such clever bambinos."

"We do make a pretty good puzzle-solving team. Eh, Pete?" asked Penny.

"For sure!" said Pete. "Besides, I bet a newspaper article would bring even more people to Pizzarelli's! Mom and Dad would like that."

Ms. Scoop nodded. "Absolutely! I'll tell everyone how amazing the pizza is! And the service isn't bad, either!" They all laughed.

The article came out that weekend. It was on the front page! The headline read PIZZA KIDS SOLVE CASE OF THE SECRET SAUCE. There was a picture of Pete and Penny in front of Pizzarelli's Pizza Parlor. Ms. Scoop wrote about how they had found clues and solved each puzzle. Then she ended with a glowing review of the pizza—as promised. She had even created a crossword puzzle based on the mystery!

"Our very own puzzle!" Pete said happily. Uncle Gio cut the crossword out of the newspaper. Then he put it in a wooden frame. He hung the puzzle up over the counter.

Redville Gazette

Crossword

Across

3. One of the first test ingredients
5. What led them to the town square
7. Boy's name
8. What fell into the sauce
10. Uncle's name

Down

1. Last name of the pizza shop owners
2. Where they make those fabulous pizzas
4. Secret in the envelope
6. Where the parents are
9. Girl's name

"Magnifico!" cried Uncle Gio.

Mr. Parcel said, "Just wait until your parents see it!"

"See what?" a voice asked from the door. Everyone looked. There were Mr. and Mrs. Pizzarelli!

"Mom! Dad! You're home!" Penny ran to hug them. Pete was right behind her.

"Hi, kids!" Mr. Pizzarelli said.

"They were very good," Uncle Gio told them. "And they are so clever!"

"They certainly are," Mr. Shears agreed. "They can solve anything!"

"Especially if it involves pizza," Elliot called out. Everybody laughed.

Mr. Pizzarelli glanced around. "Gee, business really picks up when we go away!" he joked.

"Yes," Uncle Gio agreed. "We were in the paper and everything!" He pointed to the crossword puzzle.

"I see we missed some excitement, and a puzzle or two," Mrs. Pizzarelli said, laughing. "Is somebody going to tell us what happened?"

Pete and Penny looked at each other. "We will," they promised, "but pizza comes first! Let's eat!"

Answer Page

Page 3

Page 11

Beneath yellow pitcher

Page 21

last = salt
usrag = sugar
peprep = pepper
cilrag = garlic
Vleio loi = olive oil
slabi = basil

Page 32

white pepper — 19
chili powder — 12
lemon peel — 7
sugar — 3
ginger — 15
orange juice — 23

Page 40

Page 48

PIZZARELLI

16 22 19 12 10 21 4 9 6 15
O U R K I T C H E N

Page 53

S

Keep reading!
Answer is on page 53!

Page 59

Crossword:
1 P
2 KITCHEN
3 GINGER (GIZZARELL)
4 RECIPE
5 MAZE
6 ITALY
7 PETE
8 ENVELOPE
9 PENNY
10 GIO